Another Sommer-Time Story™

Time Remote!

By Carl Sommer
Illustrated by Greg Budwine

Advance . HOUSTON
PUBLISHING, INC

Permissions
Advance Publishing, Inc.
6950 Fulton St.
Houston, TX 77022

www.advancepublishing.com

First Edition
Printed in Singapore

Library of Congress Cataloging-in-Publication Data

Sommer, Carl, 1930-
  Time remote/by Carl Sommer; illustrated by Greg Budwine.--1st ed.
    p. cm.--(Another Sommer-Time Story)
  Summary: When Christopher gets a remote controller that enables him to skip ahead in time, he tries to use it to avoid his problems.
  Cover title: Carl Sommer's Time Remote
  ISBN 1-57537-012-3 (hardcover: alk. paper). — ISBN 1-57537-064-6 (library binding: alk. paper)
  [1. Time travel Fiction. 2. Conduct of life Fiction.]
I. Budwine, Greg, ill. II. Title. III. Title: Carl Sommer's Time Remote. IV. Series: Sommer, Carl, 1930- Another Sommer-Time Story.
PZ7.S696235Ti 2000   99-16375
[E]--dc21   CIP

TiMe ReMote!

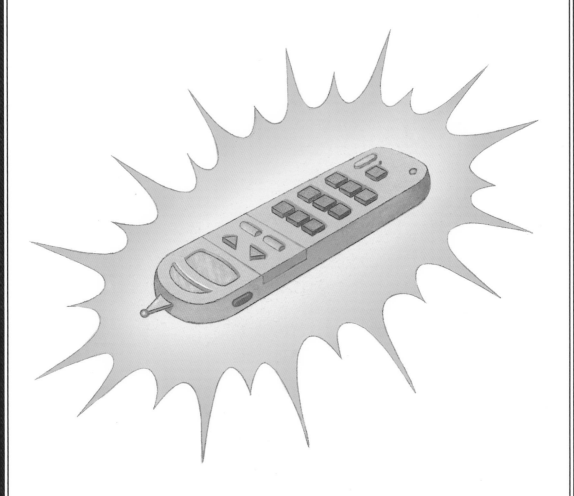

Once there was a lively and bright young boy named Christopher who had many dreams.

But sometimes he dreamed too much. Christopher would often look out the window and dream, "Ohhhhh! If only I could be outside playing instead of being inside doing all this schoolwork."

Next door to Christopher lived a kind old inventor named Dr. Finkle. Christopher loved to visit and watch him work on his different projects. One day Christopher asked him, "What are you doing today, Dr. Finkle?"

"I'm experimenting with something that

speeds up time," explained the old inventor.

Christopher's eyes popped wide open. "Speeds up time?"

"Yes," said the kind old doctor. "You dial the time you wish to skip into the remote, and zap— time goes forward."

"Wow!" said Christopher as he stared at the time remote. "Does it really work?"

Dr. Finkle rubbed his beard and frowned. "Not as I would like. I cannot make time go backwards. But I'm still working on it."

Then he smiled proudly and said, "But it works well going forward."

"It does!" said Christopher as he watched Dr. Finkle pick up the remote and start working on it.

Then Christopher said, "I wish I had that remote. I could skip doing all my homework!"

The kind old doctor stopped working. He stood, put his hand on Christopher's shoulder and said, "This time remote is only for very special occasions. It is not intended to get people out of work or out of trouble."

"Ohhhhhh!" groaned Christopher.

"Christopher," said Dr. Finkle, "didn't you say that one day you wanted to invent an—"

"Airmobile!" Christopher interrupted. "It will drive like a car and fly like an airplane."

"If you really want to do that," explained Dr. Finkle, "you'll need to work hard in school and learn to solve problems."

"I hate problems," complained Christopher, "and going to school is just one big problem!"

"Christopher!" said Dr. Finkle. "You should never say that. If you want to become successful, you must face your problems and learn from them. One day when you're flying around in your airmobile, you'll be glad you did."

But Christopher was not listening. He was dreaming again, "If only I had that time remote."

One day when Christopher was visiting Dr. Finkle, the kind old inventor said, "I'm leaving town, and I don't know when I'm coming back. Would you please feed my cat while I'm gone?"

"Sure," said Christopher. "I'll take good care of her."

"Here are the keys to the house," said Dr. Finkle. And as the kind doctor often told his friends, "If you need to borrow something while I'm gone, just help yourself."

After school the next day, Christopher went to Dr. Finkle's house to feed the cat. Just as he was leaving the house, he spotted something. He stopped in his tracks.

"Ohhhhh!" he gasped. "If only I could borrow that time remote."

Then a thought flashed through his mind, "Didn't Dr. Finkle say, 'Help yourself'?"

Without a second thought, Christopher snatched up the remote and stuffed it into his pocket.

Christopher raced to the nearby park. After making sure no one was looking, he carefully took out the time remote and began examining it.

"Oh my!" he remembered, "I'm supposed to be studying for the math test this afternoon. But if this time remote really works—"

He became so excited thinking that he might be able to skip studying for the test, that his fingers trembled as he dialed in two hours.

"I hope this works," he said as he pushed the button.

"Z-z-z-zap!" went the time remote.

Christopher looked at his watch and yelled, "It really works! It's two hours later! This is the happiest day of my life!"

Excited over his new discovery, he took off running to his house in time to hear his mother call, "Christopher! Time to eat."

When Christopher walked into the kitchen, he smelled homemade pie. "Oh, good," he said.

But when he looked at the food that Mom was cooking, he held his nose and complained, "I don't like to eat meat and vegetables."

"But they're good for you," explained Mom. "They will make you strong and healthy."

But Christopher was not listening. He walked into the living room and secretly dialed thirty minutes into his remote. He smiled as he pushed the button.

"Z-z-z-zap!" went the time remote.

"Time for dessert!" called Mom.

Christopher grinned as he headed straight for the homemade pie. "This is great!" he thought. "From now on, I'm eating only what I want!"

That night Christopher was so happy thinking about all the fun things he could do with the time remote, that he could hardly sleep.

But when he got to school the next day, his happiness quickly disappeared—he had not studied for his math test. Then his eyes lit up. "The remote! I'll just dial in a few hours—and school will be over!"

Christopher slipped the remote under his desk and dialed in the time for the dismissal bell. With a big grin he pushed the button.

"Z-z-z-zap!" went the time remote.

"Rrrrr...ing!" went the school bell.

"Great!" shouted Christopher.

As he went skipping home that afternoon, he looked at his remote and said, "Am I ever lucky! This time remote will make me the happiest person in the whole world."

The next few days and weeks went by fast. Christopher loved the time remote—it was his greatest treasure. Whenever things became hard, he used the remote. He only wanted to play.

Of course, Christopher still had problems, but not for long. He simply skipped right past them...so he thought.

The problem was—his problems were not going away—they were piling up!

Every time his mom had told him to clean his room, he had used the time remote. Now his room was a big mess.

As for school, every time he had homework or a test, he had used the time remote. Now he was failing every class.

Christopher was getting deeper and deeper
into trouble. Now he felt he had so many
problems, that there was only one way out—the
time remote.

"I'm so far behind in everything," he said to
himself, "that I'll never catch up. Besides, I'm
tired of going to school. It's time for me to be
grown-up!"

Christopher yanked the remote out of his pocket and quickly dialed more time into it than ever before! He closed his eyes as he pushed the button.

The gadget shook and spewed out great puffs of smoke. It made a terrible noise. Then all of a sudden—

"Z-z-z-z-zap!" went the time remote.

When the smoke settled, Christopher was eighteen years old!

"Yes!!!" he shouted as he walked out of the school for the last time.

He threw his books into the bushes, and said with a great big smile, "I'm so glad that my school days are over, and that my problems are gone forever! Now I can get a job and do whatever I want!"

Christopher quickly found a job working in a store stocking shelves. "This is perfect," he thought. "Now I can buy anything I want."

But Christopher soon discovered that he had more problems than before. Eating out was expensive, and he barely made enough money to pay for his apartment and car.

One day at work, Christopher began daydreaming that he was flying around in the airmobile that he had invented. Suddenly a loud voice brought him back to earth. "Christopher!" shouted his boss. "What are you doing?"

"I-I-I'm stocking shelves," he answered.

"You're doing it all wrong," the boss

complained. "You've got cans upside down and backwards, and you've mixed up the vegetables with the soups. You're going to have to be much more careful if you want to work here."

"Well!" said Christopher to himself. "If he doesn't like the way I work, I'll just find a better job. Besides, I hate this kind of work."

After work, Christopher began searching for another job. One employer asked, "What did you learn in school?" Another asked, "What kind of skills do you have?"

When he was asked questions like these, he would simply shrug his shoulders and say, "I-I-I don't know."

Since he had skipped so much school, he had hardly learned anything. All the employers told him, "We're sorry. We don't have any work for you."

Christopher continued searching for another job, but no one would hire him.

While at work, Christopher began to daydream again. He wondered if he would ever be able to build his airmobile. He shook his head and said, "You know, Dr. Finkle was right. I should have studied harder."

Then his eyes lit up. "I know what I'll do! I'll just go back to school."

Christopher began to whistle as he went to his first class in night school. But as the teacher taught, he became confused. "This is going to take lots of hard work," Christopher complained.

After two days he quit school. Christopher groaned as he went back to work stocking shelves. He hated his job and began to get even more careless.

"This is your last chance," warned the boss. "Either you improve, or you'll be fired!"

Christopher tried harder than ever to find a new job. But he had the same problem—no one would hire him because he had no skills.

As Christopher sat in his empty apartment, he reasoned, "Maybe if I were older I could get a better job."

He dialed in three years, and with great hopes he pushed the button.

"Z-z-z-zap!" went the time remote.

"Yes!!!" shouted Christopher.

But his happiness did not last long. The only job he could find was sweeping factory floors. He hated this job even more than stocking shelves!

While sweeping the floors, he noticed that the people working on machines made much more money than he did. He said to himself, "I can do that kind of work. I'll go to the office and ask the manager if I can work on the machines."

When he went to the office, the manager said, "We could use another good worker. But to work on the machines, you'll have to take a math test."

The thought of taking a test sent shivers down his spine. "Never mind," he mumbled as he picked up his broom and walked out.

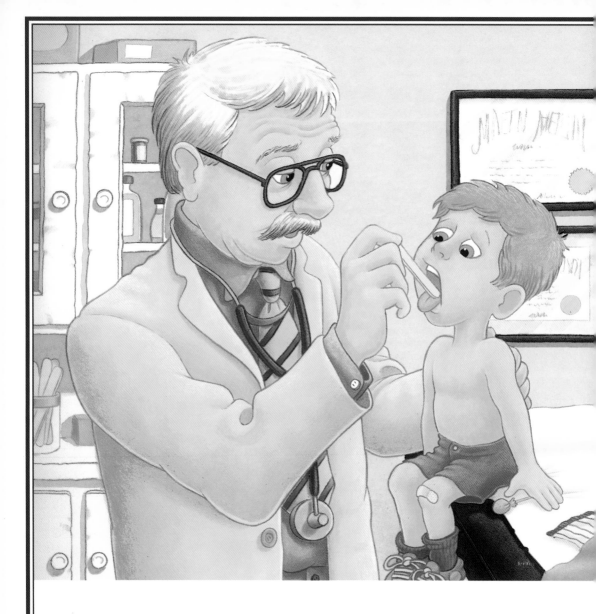

Christopher searched and searched for another job, but he always had the same problem—no one would hire him because he had no skills. Christopher became very discouraged looking for work, so he kept using the time remote to make his problems pass away.

Meanwhile, he got married and had a baby boy. Now, whenever his wife or his child became sick, and they were often sick, he would use the

time remote to make that time also pass away. His doctor advised him, "If you and your family would eat right, you would all be much healthier."

Christopher hung his head and whispered, "I know I should eat right."

But in spite of his doctor's advice, he would still use his remote whenever food was served that he did not like.

Christopher's bills began piling up. He needed more money. He searched for another job, and he finally found a nighttime job sweeping floors. He knew little else.

Now he was often sick and always tired. Life was now one Big Problem. Often he said to

himself, "Oh! How I wish I had listened to Dr. Finkle. I could have done *so* much better. If only I could go back and be in school again . . . I'd sure do things differently."

But Christopher knew that the remote could only take him forward in time, never backward.

One day while sitting in his easy chair, Christopher daydreamed of the time when he no longer had to work. "Then I can do anything *I* want," he said to himself. "Oh how I wish I were old enough so I could retire. Then I know I'd finally be happy!"

His heart began to pound for joy when he thought about all the fun things that he could do when he was retired.

Suddenly, Christopher realized that with the time remote, he could be as old as he wished! He jumped up from his chair, and without thinking any further, he quickly dialed in the time.

With a great big smile, he pushed the button. "Great!!!" he shouted as he watched the time remote rattle and sizzle and make all kinds of noises.

Then "Z-z-z-z-z-z-zap!!!" went the remote.

"Am I *ever* glad," sighed Christopher as he plopped down into his chair. "Now I don't have to work anymore."

But now Christopher had more problems than ever. He was alone. His wife had died, and his son had gotten married and moved far away. He was poor and sick, bored and sad, and had constant pain. All he did was sit in his easy chair and watch TV.

Christopher looked angrily at the remote and said, "Time went by so fast, and I enjoyed so little of it. I wish I'd never heard of a time remote. I'm throwing it away!"

Disgusted, he rose slowly from his easy chair, picked up his cane, and walked to the park. As he passed by a church, he began to shake all over as he thought about his future.

When he came to the park, he saw men and women sitting together and smiling. He saw fathers and mothers laughing and playing with their children.

"Look at me," groaned Christopher. "I've missed all the important things in life. Now I'm alone and miserable."

Christopher walked to the lake. He shook the time remote and said, "The day I got this *thing* was the worst day of my life!

"Just look at me, I've wasted my whole life. I wanted to be an inventor, but I never accomplished one good thing. Trying to live an easy life has brought me nothing but trouble and sorrow."

Shaking with anger, Christopher reached back to throw the time remote into the water— but it slipped out of his hand and smashed against a rock.

"What's this?" mumbled Christopher as he went to pick it up.

The remote had popped open, revealing a small, red button. Just then Christopher remembered how Dr. Finkle was trying to get the remote to travel backward in time. "What? What if," gasped Christopher, "Dr. Finkle was able to get this remote to work backward!!!"

His hands trembled so much that he could barely get his finger on the button. Holding his breath, he pushed the button firmly.

Suddenly, the remote shook and sizzled and made all kinds of noises. It became red hot—almost too hot to hold. Smoke began to surround Christopher.

Then "Z-z-z-z-z-z-z-zap!!!!" went the remote.

In a flash, Christopher was standing in the park, all alone. He looked at his hands, then his feet. "It worked! It really worked!" he yelled.

He jumped up and down and shouted, "Hooray!!! I'm young again! I've got another chance to live my life over. This is the happiest day of my life!"

Christopher was so happy that he raced home as fast as he could. And just as he neared his house, he heard his mother call, "Christopher! Time to eat."

Christopher hurried into the kitchen and gave his dad and mom giant hugs.

"I'm here!" he shouted as he sat down to eat. "And do I have a story to tell you! But first I need to eat my meat and vegetables."

"Are you all right?" Dad wondered.

"I'm great," laughed Christopher.

"Are you *sure* you're feeling well?" asked Mom.

"Of course!" Christopher answered. "Eating meat and vegetables makes you strong and healthy. And after I eat, I'm going to study for a math test and clean my room."

Dad and Mom were in shock. They stared at their son in amazement.

Then Christopher said, "I need to return something to Dr. Finkle's house. I don't want it anymore!"

"What is it?" asked Dad.

Christopher simply smiled and said, "A time remote."